This book belongs to:

_____Karen_____

Jane Breskin Zalben
· 1989 ·

"Oh, SIMPLE!"

STORY AND ILLUSTRATIONS BY

Jane Breskin Zalben

FARRAR · STRAUS · GIROUX New York

Copyright © 1981 Jane Breskin Zalben
All rights reserved
Published simultaneously in Canada by McGraw-Hill Ryerson Ltd., Toronto
Color separations by Princeton Polychrome Press
Printed in the United States of America by Princeton Polychrome Press
Designed by Jane Breskin Zalben
First edition, 1981
Library of Congress Cataloging in Publication Data
Zalben, Jane Breskin.   Oh, simple!
[1. Runaways—Fiction. 2. Friendship—Fiction]   I. Title.
PZ7.Z2540h   [E]   80-22587
ISBN 0-374-35604-1

To my little guy

When Beasely's father watched Monday-night football, Beasely wanted to see cartoons. So he decided to run away to Winnifred's house next door, where he thought he could get his own way.

"What are you doing here?"
"I ran away," said Beasely.
"Come on in. We'll play checkers,"
said Winnifred, "but I get the black."
Beasely won the first game.
And the second.
Winnifred made a face at him, and said,
"Well, when I ran away, I didn't
go just next door. I went to
Billie's house, three blocks over."
Beasely felt stupid.

"And when I ran away,
I didn't need a whole suitcase.
What's in yours?"
"My things."
Beasely proudly opened it.
"My best stuff is in here."

"One-piece pajamas!" squealed Winnifred.
"Those are for babies. I stopped
wearing them ages ago."

Beasely pulled out his toothbrush.
"Oh, mine's red too, but it's electric,"
said Winnifred.

"Do you want half of my candy bar?"
asked Beasely. "I only eat health
food," said Winnifred.

"Stuffed animals!" Winnifred laughed.
"I'm not afraid to sleep alone."
"Those are my slippers," said Beasely.

"Do you want to watch cartoons?" asked Beasely.
Because that's why he had run away.
"Oh, my mother doesn't let me watch cartoons.

Let's have a spelling bee," said Winnifred.
Beasely wasn't too thrilled.
"How do you spell 'elephant'?"

Beasely shifted from side to side.
"Oh, simple," said Winnifred,
"E-L-E-P-H-A-N-T."
"Can you spell 'acrobatic'?"
Beasely stared at the ceiling.
"Oh, simple," she said, smiling.
"A-C-R-O-B-A-T-I-C! How do you spell
'antidisestablishmentarianism'?"
Beasely looked blankly at her.
"Oh, SIMPLE!" she said smugly.

"That does it!" shouted Beasely.
"I wouldn't stay here for all the
cartoons in the whole world.
You're a real boss!"
Beasely stuffed everything back
into his suitcase. Winnifred yelled,
"Take those dumb, yucky frog slippers with
you. Get them off my good bedspread!"

Beasely dragged his suitcase back home.

His father was almost asleep in his chair.

"Good night, Dad. I love you," he whispered.

"I love you, too, peanut."

Beasely plopped down on his bed.

He was even too tired to take off his sneakers.

The next morning, the front doorbell rang.
It was Winnifred. "Hi, Beasely.
You forgot your dinosaur book."
"Do you want to eat breakfast?"
asked Beasely. "Well, okay,"
said Winnifred shyly.
"I'm making pancakes," he said.
"Do you know how?"
"No," said Winnifred.

"Oh, SIMPLE!" said Beasely.